Teddy and Oso
Christmas Stories

Two Christmas Stories Featuring Teddy and Oso

D1557749

Teddy and Oso Decorate the Christmas Tree

Story by Peggy Sandmann
Illustrated by Mark Sandmann

Teddy and Oso's Favorite
Things to do Over Christmas Vacation

Story by Peggy and Mark Sandmann
Illustrated by Mark Sandmann

For Graham, Alexandrea, Charlotte, Mia, Jayden, Fredrick, Abigail, Lily, and Ferdinand

Teddy and Oso

Decorate the Christmas Tree

Story By: Peggy Sandmann

Illustrated by: Mark Sandmann

This is the first Christmas that Teddy and Oso are together as friends.

They were each welcomed into the home of Mark and Peggy over the last two years.

Teddy thought that it would be fun to get Oso to help him decorate the Christmas tree for the family get-together.

Oso is not sure how he can help. But he will do the best that he could for Teddy and the family!

Oso started to look around the living room. No Christmas tree! "Teddy, Teddy! Where did you put the Christmas tree?"

"It is still in the woods!", said Teddy.

So they went out into the woods to pick a tree.

They found a nice big one and cut it down.

Now the tree was in the woods but it needed to be in the house.

So they pulled and tugged and heaved and hauled until it was in the house and they set it up in the living room!

First Teddy and Oso made sure that the tree was straight up and down on the stand.

Then they went up to the attic to look for the box of Christmas tree stuff.

They found a lot of other stuff.

They found a very old wedding dress, a potty chair, a box of books, some suitcases, and the box of Christmas decorations.

Getting the box down the stairs was a big challenge for them!

Teddy thought working together was better than last year. Then he did not have his friend from Spain and had to move the box all by himself.

Oso was thinking: "Es divertido trabajar con Teddy"(it is fun to work with Teddy).

Teddy and Oso picked up a string of beads and went around the tree.

Teddy turned around and saw that the tree was tipping over. "Oh No! The treeeee!", he shouts as he tried to catch the tree.

After the tree was back up they agreed that maybe they needed to talk about what they were doing so they don't pull the tree down again.

Oso thought that it would be fun for each to have a different colored string of beads.

"You have the red beads because you have a red shirt, and I will take the blue beads because I have a blue shirt."

Things went much better this time.

After the beads were up Teddy said; "Now to get the decorations on the tree!"

"What is with all of the bells?" Oso asked.

Teddy pointed to his shirt.

Oso looked at his shirt and was confused. "What would your shirt have anything to do with bells?"

Teddy said, " I have a bell on my shirt! And Peggy likes to play hand bells

"Ohhhh! Si. Yo Comprendo! Gracias, Teddy!" Said Oso. "Hand bells make a very pretty sound."

"Yes", said Teddy, they do.

Teddy and Oso each picked up more decorations and placed them on the tree.

Teddy started to sing the Christmas song, Silent Night. Oso joined in, with the Spanish version, Noche de Paz.

It sounded funny with them singing in two languages at once.

They decided that it would be more fun to make up a song about them trimming the tree together.

Today is the day that we trim the tree,

working together, just you and me.

The tree to be trimmed by two little bears

is pulled slowly up the outside stairs.

Together we set it up straight to the top

Then we almost made it go plop

Decorate we, with shine and hue

brother bears from countries two.

When they were done with the decorations they stood back and admired the tree.

Feliz Navidad, Said Teddy.

Merry Christmas, Said Oso.

Teddy and Osos's

Favorite Things to do Over Christmas Vacation

Story By: Peggy and Mark Sandmann

Illustrated by: Mark Sandmann

We asked Teddy and Oso What they like to do on Christmas vacation. This is what they said:

 Teddy and I like to eat bearies! We really like it when the beary juice dribbles down our chin! We even have contests to see who can get the longest dribble down their neck!

 Oso! That is something that we do in the summer. We are supposed to say something about what we like to do on our Christmas Vacation!

 Oh that is different. Let us talk about the things we have been doing since school let out.

 That sounds like a good way to start.

Teddy and I like to go sledding. I sit in the back and Teddy sits in the front. He is really good at steering the toboggan so we don't hit trees.

We go down the hill really fast and the snow flies high in the air. Oso is very good at steering too but he doesn't like getting all the snow in his face.

Peggy sometimes will make us hot chocolate for a warm treat after sledding. We like to drink it outside because the steam makes little clouds.

Don't forget the marshmallows. Everyone knows hot chocolate is better with marshmallows. Sometimes I get the melted marshmallow stuck under my nose.

We sing Christmas Carols with friends on cold winter nights. The group lets me sing Silent Night with Teddy the way I learned it in Spain. There it is called Noche De Paz.

That means Night of Peace. Oso and I sing it quietly and peacefully. After we are done some people give us cookies. We both love cookies.

Speaking of cookies. Oso and I love to make cookies when the weather is too bad to go outside and play. I think chocolate chip cookies are the best.

We even have our own teddy bear sized oven in the kitchen where we bake our cookies. I am happy to help Teddy eat his chocolate chip cookies.

After baking cookies we like to play board games in the living room. We bring milk and our cookies with us and have a great time.

We play the same games that most children and families like to play. Our favorite game is called Bear Trails and we can play it all day long.

Even when the weather is really cold we love to go downhill skiing. I like the wind going through my fur when I go back and forth on the hillside.

I like riding on the chair lift. I can see things far away when I am up high. Little bears like us don't get to see over things very often.

Ice skating at the frozen pond can be very fun if you can keep from falling down. I like to go fast so I can feel the wind on my nose.

I like to go slower so I can do spins and jumps. I fall down sometimes because I am always trying a new trick.

Some nights we can stay up and watch the Christmas specials on TV. A Christmas Carol can get real scary so we only watch it when Peggy or Mark are with us.

 I like the Christmas special that only shows the children. When Peggy makes us watch It's a Wonderful Life we both fall asleep before it is done.

A Christmas time snowfall is the best for making a snow man. The snow is sticky and it is easy to make snowballs.

 Oso and I roll the bottom part as a team. Then I roll the middle while Oso makes the head. We work together to pile up the snowballs. It is good to have a brother.

The best part of Christmas vacation
is spending good time with the family
we love

Made in the USA
Monee, IL
30 July 2020